Keep Climbing, Girls

By Beah E. Richards
Illustrated by R. Gregory Christie
Introduction by LisaGay Hamilton

Simon & Schuster Books for Young Readers
New York London Toronto Sydney

SIMON & SCHUSTER BOOKS FOR YOUNG READERS
An imprint of Simon & Schuster Children's Publishing Division
1230 Avenue of the Americas, New York, New York 10020

First Simon & Schuster edition, 2006

Book design by Einav Aviram
The text for this book is set in Myriad Tilt.
The illustrations for this book are rendered in gouache.
Manufactured in China
2 4 6 8 10 9 7 5 3
Library of Congress Cataloging-in-Publication Data
Richards, Beah E.
Keep climbing, girls / Beah E. Richards ; introduction by LisaGay Hamilton ; illustrated by R. Gregory Christie.
p. cm.
ISBN-13: 978-1-4169-0264-5
ISBN-10: 1-4169-0264-3 (hardcover)
1. Girls—Juvenile poetry. 2. Conduct of life—Juvenile poetry. 3. Children's poetry, American.
I. Christie, Gregory, 1971– ill. II. Title.
PS3568.I31515K44 2005
811'.54—dc22 2004029153

With my respect to the ever-resilient Denise Poche-Jetter,
and to every female that continues onward and upward through life
with intrepidity, wisdom, and kindness—R. G. C.

This book is dedicated to Paul Coates, for his wisdom; to my son, Azizi, for his very being; to all the beautiful children of Vicksburg, Mississippi, past, present, and future; and to Beah E. Richards, my African Teacher, who opened my eyes, deepened my thoughts, and continues to fill me with love and courage.—L. H.

Acknowledgments

Beah always said that great fortune came from the love of family and good friends. Beah felt forever grateful for her niece, Sherry Fisher Greene. It was Sherry who cared for Beah in her home the last four months of her life. Clearly this book would not have been possible without the beautiful and inspirational words of Beah E. Richards and the continued love, trust, and friendship that Miss Fisher has shown for me. I would also like to thank my sister, Heidi Hamilton, for her legal counsel; Lynda Wright, who has always been there for me at crunch time; and to my assistant, KayLyn Byrne, for her loyalty and friendship.—L. H.

Introduction

I grew up watching Beah Richards perform in films and on television. Even in the limited roles Hollywood offered African-American women throughout her career—almost always maids and old ladies—each of Beah's portrayals personified grace, dignity, and artistry. I could never forget a single performance. Her talent was undeniable in such films as *Guess Who's Coming to Dinner* and *In the Heat of the Night* , or during her many guest appearances on television shows like *Frank's Place* and *Sanford and Son.*

In 1996 I had the honor of working with Beah on the film *Beloved,* directed by Jonathan Demme. Over the next few years she and I forged an extraordinary bond. Beah became my friend, mentor, and inspiration. I was amazed to learn of her accomplishments as a poet, a teacher, a dancer, and a political activist, and of her lifelong commitment to the African-American community and to all oppressed people.

Beah's depth and skill as a poet and an actor placed her alongside great African-American social activists like Paul Robeson and William and Louise Patterson. On the same stage with these warriors and others, Beah performed her poetry at concerts and political rallies around the country throughout her career.

Her only published collection of poetry entitled, *A Black Woman Speaks,* addresses all things concerned with love—love of self, and love of humanity. "Keep Climbing, Girls" is a part of that volume. How perfect it is that Beah wrote this ode to all human beings, young and old, male and female, encouraging us to reach far beyond the expectations society might have for us.

Before Beah's death in 2000 she and I began collaborating on a documentary about her life, *Beah: A Black Woman Speaks.* (With the help of Jonathan Demme and HBO, our film was completed in 2003.) At the close of the documentary, Beah looks directly into the camera and emphatically states,"The world you want to create needs you. It needs you to create it. It needs to hear what you have to say. The last word has not been spoken!"

Just as in "Keep Climbing, Girls," Beah is challenging each of us to fight for a world that embraces freedom and equality for all. We must do this with love of self and love for all. We must do this with determination—"Climbing right up to the toppermost bough of the very tallest tree . . . letting no one prevent us."

LisaGay Hamilton

January 2006

You could tell by the way Miss Nettie stood,
hands on her hips,
and on her forehead an unbelieving frown,
the words she was about to speak
would indeed be profound.

“Come down out o’ that tree
before you break your neck,” she said.
“Come down!”
Then she’d whirl right round through the door,
confident that she need say no more.

But Miss Nettie hadn't reckoned with
a little girl's ambition.
(One that she must satisfy
at the risk of extreme contrition.)

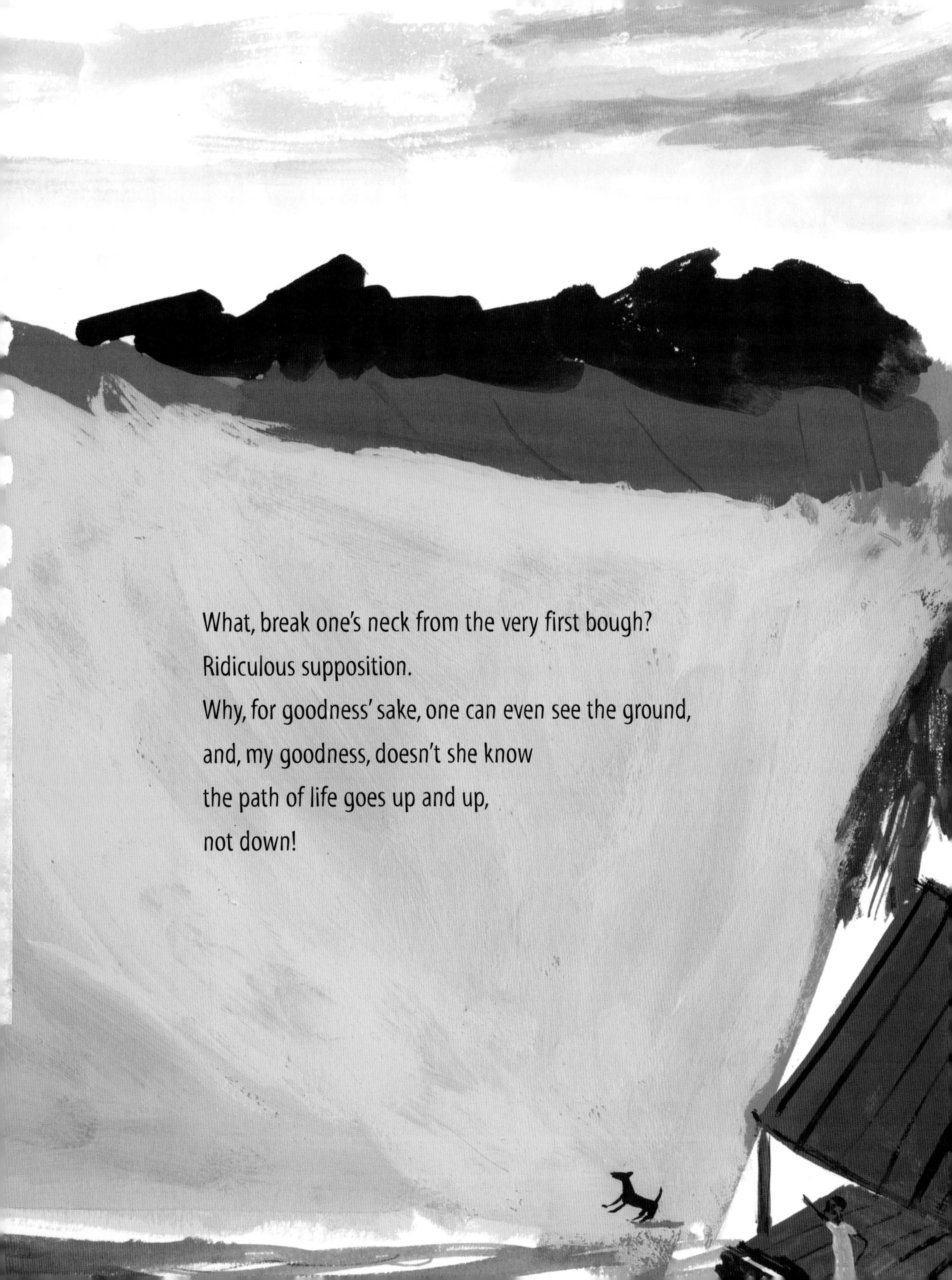

What, break one's neck from the very first bough?
Ridiculous supposition.
Why, for goodness' sake, one can even see the ground,
and, my goodness, doesn't she know
the path of life goes up and up,
not down!

Miss Nettie pops out again
to view the situation.
Over her face there comes this time
a look of consternation.

"You see that child's ignoring me.
Climbed right up to the middle of that tree!"
(Obviously this requires diplomacy.)

"All right," she said, using the blade of shame.
"You're no little girl," she said,
showing her disdain.

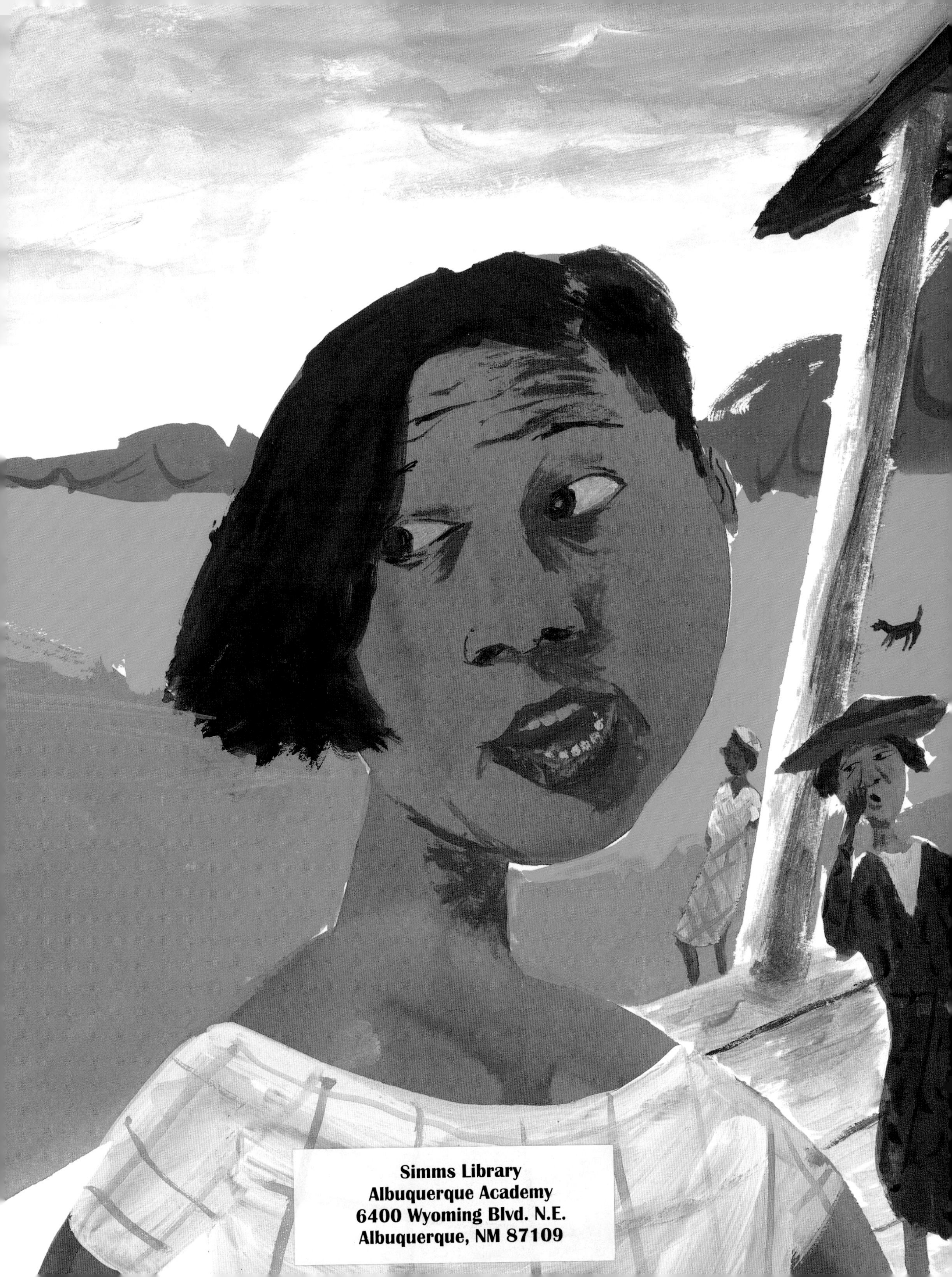

"You're a tomboy, that's what you are,
and you're going to have a tomboy's scars."
Then with a mighty flourish
she'd whirl right round through the door,
confident that she need say no more.

But Miss Nettie hadn't reckoned with the wisdom
of little girls.
For even they know little boys have the upper hand
in this world.

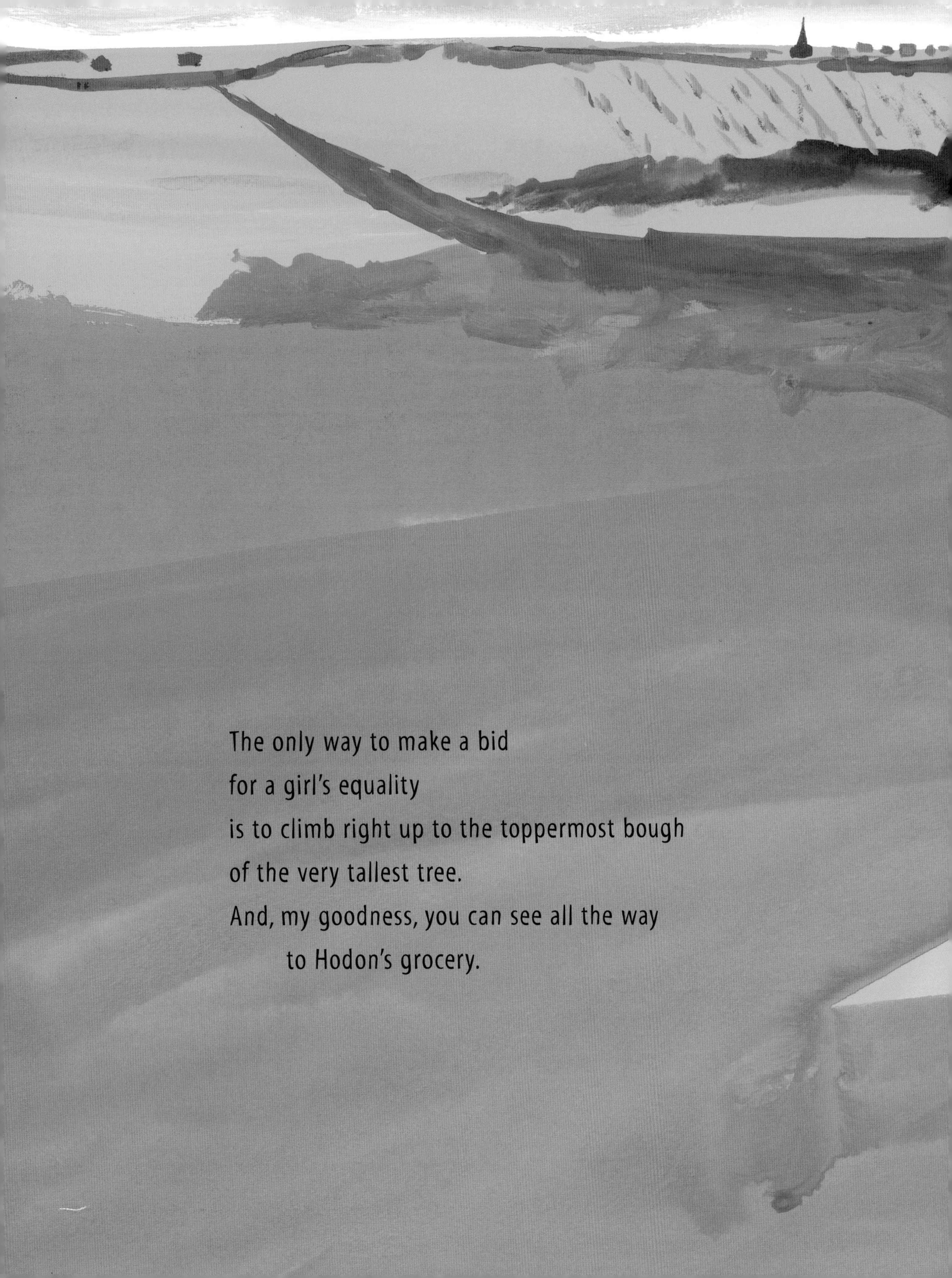

The only way to make a bid
for a girl's equality
is to climb right up to the toppermost bough
of the very tallest tree.
And, my goodness, you can see all the way
to Hodon's grocery.

Miss Nettie hurries out again
and shouts out angrily,
"Come down from there, right now,"
she says,
(her voice tight with fear).
"Come down from there right this minute
or I'll break your neck, you hear!"

But a little girl victorious
can't hide her childish glee,
to see Miss Nettie so put out
that she, a girl, could climb a tree.

Though the braids be pulled,
and the ear be tweaked,
t'won't dim the brave adventure.

The moral is: Keep climbing, girls,
and let no one prevent you!